‖‖‖ ‖ ‖‖‖‖‖‖‖‖ ‖‖ ‖ ‖‖‖‖‖ ‖‖‖ ‖‖‖‖ ‖‖‖‖ ‖ ‖‖‖
W9-BER-504

0 8 3 4

THE
WATER
WITCH

SUSANNAH BRIN

TAKE TEN BOOKS

BY SUSANNAH BRIN

CHILLERS

THRILLERS

Development and Production: Laurel Associates, Inc.
Cover Illustrator: Black Eagle Productions

© 1998 Saddleback Publishing, Inc.

SADDLEBACK
PUBLISHING • INC.

3505 Cadillac Ave., Building F-9
Costa Mesa, CA 92626

ISBN 1-56254-236-2

Printed in the United States of America
03 02 01 MM 01 00 CM 99 98 8 7 6 5 4 3 2 1

CONTENTS

Chapter 1

Jimmy Brade stretched out his legs and tried to relax. His headache was pounding like a jackhammer. He glanced over at his friend, Harley Smith. Harley sat hunched behind the steering wheel, his eyes glued to the road. Jimmy thought he looked like a grownup Huckleberry Finn.

"How you doing, buddy?" asked Harley, looking back at Jimmy.

"Great. Just great," Jimmy lied. Harley grinned. "It won't be long now," he said. "In another twenty minutes we'll be in River Junction."

Jimmy nodded. He didn't feel like talking. He wanted to close his eyes and go to sleep. But he could feel

Harley watching him, trying to figure out if he was *really* okay.

It had been three months since the car accident. It bugged Jimmy that everyone acted like he was made of glass, like he was going to self-destruct at any minute. He was *fine*. It was only a headache. A normal headache. He rubbed his forehead. His long fingers touched the scar that snaked from his eyebrow to his hairline. Harley said the scar gave Jimmy's face character. But Jimmy wasn't so sure. To him it just looked red and ugly.

Harley switched on the truck's radio. Faint sounds of music could be heard between patches of crackling static. Disgusted, Harley turned the radio off. "I should've put a tape deck in this rig," grumbled Harley.

"Yeah. I was going to put a CD player in my jeep," Jimmy said. "I still might when I get a new one."

"I wouldn't think that you'd want another jeep after what happened," said Harley, glancing over at Jimmy with surprise.

"Why not?"

"Well, shoot, man! You almost *died*. They had to cut you out of that tin can to save your life."

"So?"

"So, I think you should buy something big and safe," said Harley.

"Like *this* bucket of bolts?" laughed Jimmy.

"Wait a minute, you're talking about my pride and joy. This here baby is one fine machine. It's got a V-8 engine, four-wheel drive, steel-reinforced body. It's safe and it's fast," said Harley, proudly. Grinning, he stomped down on the gas pedal. The truck shot forward up the hill.

Jimmy's hand curled tightly around his seatbelt. The hum of the pickup's tires seemed to roar in his ears. The sound made the pain in his head throb faster and faster. He glanced at the speedometer, but he couldn't read it. The numbers seemed to blur. "Slow down, Harley!" Jimmy yelled. Fear edged his voice.

Startled, Harley eased up on the gas. "I'm only going sixty, man."

"Go forty." Jimmy rolled down his window. Cold night air rushed into the cab. It was just like the night of the accident. Jimmy had been on the freeway, thinking about changing lanes. Then suddenly a car had appeared in front of him. The car was going the wrong way! Jimmy swerved to the right, but it was too late. The other car slammed head-on into him. The impact flipped the jeep over an embankment.

"Are you hungry?" Harley asked, breaking Jimmy's thoughts.

"No."

"I'm starved. If a bear walked across the road right now, I think I'd have to kill it and eat it," Harley joked. Then he reached down and felt along the floor under his feet.

"What are you doing?" asked Jimmy.

"Looking for that sack with the candy bars in it," said Harley, glancing from the road to the floor and back to the road again.

Then suddenly a car came out of nowhere, its lights on high beam. It rounded the curve and headed toward them. Blinded by the lights, Jimmy thought the car was coming straight at them. His body tensed, anticipating the impact. Without thinking, he grabbed the steering wheel and yanked it to the right. The pickup swerved and skidded sideways.

"What are you doing, man? Are you trying to get us killed?" yelled Harley, shoving Jimmy away roughly. "Get your hands off the wheel!"

Gravel sprayed against the sides of the pickup as it headed for a ditch. Quickly, Harley turned the wheel and stepped on the gas. The truck fishtailed in the loose gravel, but Harley finally got it under control and it bumped back onto the road. Harley was angry. "What did you think you were doing back there?" he growled.

Jimmy shuddered. He could feel his heart racing. "That car was headed straight for us."

Harley shook his head. "No way! It wasn't anywhere *near* the white line, Jimmy."

Jimmy looked down at his lap. His hand still clutched the seatbelt buckle. "You didn't really see it," Jimmy sputtered. "You were looking for the candy bars, remember?"

Harley didn't say anything more,

but his face looked sad. It made Jimmy angry. He didn't want his friend's pity or concern. He didn't need it. He knew what he had seen. The car had been headed *straight for them.*

Turning away from Harley, Jimmy stared out the window. Up ahead, he could see a road sign. The letters looked blood red against the black sky. *River Junction* is what the sign said.

Chapter 2

Jimmy wiped the sweat from his forehead. Looking up, he watched his friend wading toward him, across the shallow rapids of the river. Two large trout hung from a metal stringer in Harley's hand.

"Hey, Jimmy, I got two more!" yelled Harley, holding up the trout like trophies. "Look at these beauties."

Crouching down, Harley took the trout from the string on his belt. He placed his recent catch with the other fat trout lying in the grass. "They're really biting today. I can't believe you haven't caught one yet," he said, flopping down next to Jimmy.

"I had a couple of nibbles. But I've spent most of the time untangling my line. There sure is a lot of trash in this river," said Jimmy.

Harley frowned. "You can't go anywhere anymore without stepping on somebody's garbage. It makes me sick." He stood up and stared out at the river, shaking his head.

"Well, I think I'll wade on down the river and see what I can find," Harley said. He picked up his pole and waited for Jimmy to join him. "You coming?"

"Go ahead. I'm tired. I think I'll just find me a nice big rock to sit on."

"You've been doing too much sitting lately. You need to get physical, buddy. Might be good to shut down your brain for a while," advised Harley.

Jimmy knew his friend was just trying to help—but he didn't *need* help. Sure, he'd been a little wacko after his accident. For a few weeks, he couldn't remember who he was or what had happened. It was frightening. But all the doctors had assured him that sometimes that could happen—especially after a head injury.

"If you want to catch fish, you've got to get in the water and track them down. You can't catch fish sitting on a rock," said Harley, starting back toward the river.

"Oh, yeah? Want to bet? I've got five bucks that says I can," challenged Jimmy. He reached into his pocket and pulled out a handful of bills.

Harley's brown eyes sparkled with amusement. "You know I can't resist a bet. You're on!"

Jimmy watched as Harley stepped back into the river and started making his way downstream. He congratulated himself on his cleverness. That little bet had gotten Harley off his case. Now he could kick back and relax. Picking up his fishing pole, he waded upstream toward an outcropping of giant gray boulders. The cold, greenish-blue water swirled around his ankles and splashed against his bare legs.

After a few minutes, Jimmy climbed up on a boulder and sat down. The rock was warm from the sun, and the heat felt good on his legs. He looked around. A *perfect* spot, he thought, dropping his line into the deep pool of water. Beyond the pool, a series of narrow rapids raged fast and hard.

Harley had warned him that the rapids were dangerous and deadly. But Jimmy wasn't worried. He didn't plan on getting anywhere near the rapids. He leaned on his side and gazed at his fishing line bobbing gently in the pool. The afternoon sun was hot. He closed his eyes and listened to the water lapping against the boulder.

Jimmy was half asleep when he heard a yell. When he opened his eyes he saw a gun strapped to a leg. He sat up with a start.

"Not a safe place to be sleeping, boy. You could roll right into the water," warned a potbellied man wearing a sheriff's badge.

"I wasn't asleep, just resting my eyes," lied Jimmy.

"Uh huh," said the sheriff, holding out his hand. "The name is Ray Cox."

"I'm Jimmy Brade, Mr. Cox," said Jimmy, grasping the man's hand. "Call me Ray," said the sheriff.

The sheriff seemed friendly enough, but Jimmy wondered what he wanted. He hadn't broken any laws—at least none that he knew of. "I've got a fishing license. Do you want to see it?"

Ray Cox laughed. "I'm the sheriff, son, not the game warden. I'm looking for Harley Smith. I heard he was up here using his parents' cabin. His daddy and I go way back," said Ray, grinning. Only his eyes, small, quick, and probing, betrayed the cunning brain behind his friendly face.

Jimmy hesitated, then pointed to a figure standing in the river about five hundred yards downstream.

"I should've known that was him, wading the stream. That's the best way to fish for trout," Ray said, glancing at the deep pool of water where Jimmy's line bobbed gently. The sheriff stared at the water for a long time.

Jimmy laughed. "That's what he told me. Harley believes in tracking the fish like they were deer or something."

"You aren't going to catch anything in this pool, son. The water may look calm and peaceful, but there's a mean undertow down there. Better fishing downstream," said the sheriff. His eyes looked nervous.

"I think I'll just try my luck right here a while," Jimmy said. The sheriff shot him a sharp look, then shrugged. "Suit yourself. But if you want to catch the big ones, go down below the rapids. After running the rapids, the fish rest a spell, see? So that's a good place to drop your line."

Jimmy smiled. "I'll remember that, sheriff—I mean, Ray."

The older man frowned. "Guess I'll go down and say hello to Harley." Before walking off, he stared down into the pool again for a few long moments. Jimmy didn't know what to make of the strange look on his face.

Chapter 3

Shadows grew and spread out across the river like bloodstains on a cotton shirt. Jimmy looked down the river in Harley's direction. Harley was alone. The sheriff must have left. An hour had passed, and he still hadn't gotten one nibble. He sighed. *The sheriff is probably right,* he thought. *There aren't any fish in this pool.*

Jimmy leaned over the edge of the boulder and gazed into the water. It looked like a black hole, deep and mysterious. Then a flash of gold caught his eye. Quickly, he rolled onto his stomach and reached for the golden object. As his fingers tightened around it, he realized that it was a ring. And then he realized that the ring was attached to a hand!

Jimmy's stomach heaved. Jerking his hand out of the water, he studied the shiny gold ring that lay in his palm. Somehow, when his hand had shot upward, the ring had slipped off the finger. Jimmy swallowed hard to keep from throwing up. He'd never seen a dead body before. Forcing himself to look back down into the pool, he saw nothing. The hand had disappeared!

Jimmy didn't know what to do. Again, he looked at the ring. It was so small and delicately made that it must be a woman's ring. The face of the ring was designed in the shape of two tiny hands. The hands were clutching a heart. Overhead, a hawk flapped its wings and glided low over the water. As Jimmy watched it, he heard something splash in the pool.

Jimmy slipped the ring onto his little finger. The gold felt cold against his skin. He thought about the hand in the water. Was it just a hand—or was there a whole body floating down there? He shivered.

Jumping quickly down onto another boulder, Jimmy tried to get a closer look. Smooth, grayish-white rocks surrounded the pool. The river charged at the rocks in a frenzy, boiling its way between the rocks until it trickled into the deep, dark, still pool. The calm appearance of the pool's water was deceptive, Jimmy realized. Underneath the surface lurked a powerful, sucking maw that could pull a person down to the depths.

Working his way around the edge of the pool, Jimmy didn't see anything unusual. Glancing downstream, he saw Harley working his way toward him. He waved at his friend. Then, out of the corner of his eye, he saw a flash of something long and silvery.

Jimmy stared at the water, his

mouth hanging open. A *woman* was floating just beneath the surface! She was the most beautiful woman he'd ever seen. She was dressed in a long, sequined gown of the thinnest silk. Blond hair, the color of ripe wheat, fanned out around her shoulders. Her blue eyes were open wide.

Jimmy crouched down, waiting for the woman's body to drift closer to the rocks. Straining to see past the murky shadows, he leaned farther out from the rock. Then he slipped and hit the water hard. Air rushed out of his lungs, and he panicked. All of a sudden he had forgotten how to swim! Thrashing his arms in the water, he felt something wrapping itself around his legs. Before Jimmy knew it, he was pulled down into the darkness.

Don't let me drown, Jimmy prayed as he struggled to break free. He thrust his hands toward the surface, hoping to find something to grab onto. Finally, with his lungs ready to burst, he kicked at the thing tangled around his feet. Released from its hold, he shot up to the surface. In a moment he was gulping for air and screaming for help. But no one seemed to hear him.

Jimmy swam from rock to rock, searching for a handhold. But the rocks were too smooth and slippery.

Then, without warning, he felt himself being pulled down again. The swirling water sucked him deeper and deeper. He struggled against the unseen force. Then his foot hit on a small indentation in a rock. He jammed his toes into the space and struggled to pull his body close to the rock. Luckily, he found a few tiny fingerholds.

Jimmy inched his body up the rock until his head was out of the water. When he looked around, he saw Harley running toward him.

"Help me!" Jimmy screamed. His arms shook with exhaustion, and he could barely catch his breath. Then he could feel something soft brushing against his legs and curling around his ankles. Jimmy's feet slipped from the rock, and he went down again.

Chapter 4

Jimmy could feel Harley's strong hands grabbing his arms and pulling him upward. He felt his body scraping against the rocks as his friend dragged him to safety. For a long time, Jimmy lay face down on the boulder. He was exhausted. Water dripped from his hair and his nose and mouth. After a few minutes, he coughed and sat up.

"What happened, man?" asked Harley, his voice full of concern. "Did you slip, or what?"

Jimmy took a deep breath. "Yeah, I guess that's what happened. I was trying to get a better look at the body— and the next thing I knew I was in the water, fighting for my life."

"What are you talking about? *What* body?" Harley gasped.

"There's a dead woman in the pool, Harley. I don't know how long she's been down there. But she is beautiful, man—really beautiful. She has long blond hair and a face like an angel."

Harley's mouth dropped open. He stared hard at Jimmy.

"She was wearing some kind of . . . evening dress. It sparkled," said Jimmy.

"Maybe she was going to a pool party," joked Harley, nervously.

"I'm serious!" snapped Jimmy. "We've got to notify the police." Shivering, he looked downstream at the churning river rapids.

Harley put his arm around his friend's shoulders. "Come on. You need to get out of those wet clothes."

Jimmy shook free of Harley's arm. "I *know* what I saw."

"I know you *think* you saw something. But if a girl drowned in that pool, she'd have been dragged down the river a long time ago," said Harley, gently. "Look, I want to show you something." Grabbing a large stick, he threw it into the pool. The stick floated for one or two seconds, and then it disappeared under the water.

"So?"

"Just keep your eyes on that open patch of water," Harley said. He pointed to a place beyond the cluster of boulders. In a few minutes Jimmy saw the stick surface farther downriver.

Silently, Jimmy pushed past Harley and walked away. It didn't make sense. Harley was right. Jimmy had seen with his own eyes how the stick was sucked down and then out into the river. But he'd also seen the blond.

"Go get warm. I'll get the gear," yelled Harley.

Jimmy walked over to the pickup. He found an old sweatshirt behind the seat and put it on. Rubbing his hands against his arms, he couldn't remember ever being so cold.

Harley threw their gear into the back of the truck and slid behind the wheel. He started the pickup's engine and turned the heater to high. "Where'd you get that ring?"

Jimmy glanced at the ring on his little finger. He'd forgotten all about it. "This ring belongs to the woman in the pool," he explained.

"I'm not following you, buddy."

"I saw a flash of gold in the water. When I grabbed for it, I didn't know it was a ring. And I sure didn't know it was attached to a hand," explained Jimmy. "When I looked at what I was holding, I freaked out. Then, when I yanked my hand back, I saw that the ring was in it."

"You *sure* you didn't find it near the riverbank?" Harley asked.

"No." Jimmy patiently repeated the sequence of events. Finally, he quit talking, quit trying to convince Harley. It was obvious from the look on his friend's face that he didn't believe a word Jimmy had said.

"It doesn't matter where you found it, okay? It's a nice ring," said Harley.

Jimmy didn't say anything.

"It's an Irish friendship ring," said Harley, trying to ease the tension. "The clasped hands signify friendship. And the heart symbolizes the love shared between two friends."

Jimmy was surprised by his friend's poetic description of the ring. Harley always tried to be so macho. Jimmy had never suspected that his friend might have a softer side. "How do you know?" asked Jimmy.

"My mom had one. She wore it until Dad got her a fancy diamond for their anniversary," said Harley. Jimmy fingered the ring with his thumb and thought about what Harley had said. Out on the river, silver sequins glistened white against the darkness.

It was after ten when the pickup pulled in to the tiny tavern next to the diner. Harley wanted to shoot some pool. Jimmy went along with the idea. He figured he owed Harley one, for agreeing to eat at the diner. Harley had wanted to eat the trout he'd caught. In fact, he'd talked of nothing else on the ride back to the cabin. But when Jimmy had suggested they get hamburgers instead, Harley quickly agreed.

Jimmy guessed his friend realized that fish was the last thing he wanted to eat. And he was right. Even now, just thinking about dead fish made his stomach churn.

"How about a dollar a game?" asked Harley as he racked up the balls.

"That's a little steep, don't you think?" said Jimmy. He took a pool cue from the wall and chalked the tip.

Harley grinned mischievously. "Just thought you might want to win back that fiver you lost earlier today."

Jimmy laughed. "Okay. You want to break?"

"Go ahead. That way I can choose what I want," teased Harley, implying that Jimmy wouldn't be able to sink a ball on the break.

Jimmy took his shot. The white cueball slammed into the other balls, sending two solid-colored balls into the corner pocket. Harley shrugged and said, "Beginner's luck!" Jimmy slowly shot ball after ball into the pockets. After sinking all of the balls, he straightened up and smiled at Harley. "You know something? Pool is the only ball sport I'm good at."

Harley handed Jimmy a dollar and started racking the balls again. "You just got lucky that time."

"Right!" Jimmy laughed and sat down on a stool to wait his turn. He looked around and noticed a pretty woman with long blond hair standing by the jukebox. He watched her drop a quarter into the machine and punch a button. A country western song about lost love started up, adding to the noise in the room.

Harley sank three balls, then missed. As Jimmy stepped up to take his turn, he looked back over at the young woman. She was swaying to the music. *How odd*, Jimmy thought. *Something about her seems strangely familiar.*

Jimmy lost that game and the next one. He could hear Harley crowing with delight, but he couldn't take his eyes off the young woman at the jukebox. As Harley racked up the balls for the fourth game, Jimmy saw the blond woman getting ready to leave. She glanced in his direction and smiled.

Without a word to his friend, Jimmy handed his cue to a man who'd been waiting to play. Then he hurried after the young woman.

Chapter 5

The main street of River Junction was deserted. A naked light bulb hung from a utility pole at one end of the street. Jimmy searched the darkness. He didn't see the blond woman anywhere. Where could she have gone?

River Junction was a small town, barely a dot on the map. He wondered if she had turned down Summer's Road. He hoped not. Summer's Road was a maze of driveways and little paths. All of them led through the woods to the summer homes and cabins built along the river. Jimmy climbed the steps to the diner and peeked in the window. The place was empty. Then he heard a soft voice say, "The diner is closed."

Startled, Jimmy spun around. The blond woman had appeared out of nowhere. Now she was leaning against a light pole. She was dressed all in white—white sweater, white skirt, white sandals. "Nice night for a walk," she said. Her voice was as sweet and haunting as a melody.

Jimmy stared at her in disbelief. How beautiful she was! Like a princess right out of a storybook. Suddenly embarrassed, he managed to mumble that it was a nice night.

"Are you on vacation?" she asked.

"Yeah. I mean yes. I'm here with my friend Harley. His parents have a place by the river. We came up to fish and relax and spend a bit of time together before we start college in the fall." The words poured out of his mouth in one long rush. Jimmy was afraid she could hear his heart beating. To him it sounded louder than a drum.

"That's nice." She smiled.

"Are you vacationing, too?" he asked, trying to think of something to keep the conversation going.

She laughed. "I suppose you could call it that."

He laughed, too, feeling like he was back in high school on a first date. She walked toward him. Her long blond hair, the color of ripe wheat, swirled around her shoulders as she walked. Even though the night was dark, Jimmy could see the blue of summer in her eyes. The idea that he'd met her before still tugged at the back of his mind.

"My name is Jim Brade, but all my friends call me Jimmy." He smiled shyly at her and shifted his weight from one foot to the other.

"I'm Lisa," she said, offering him her hand.

When he took it in his, her hand felt icy cold. She lifted his hand closer to her face and admired the ring on his finger. "I had a ring like that once."

"It's an Irish friendship ring. The clasped hands stand for friendship," Jimmy explained.

"I know. Some of the Irish believe that the ring binds the giver and the wearer of the ring together in a circle of love that lasts forever. They share the same heart, you see," said Lisa, pointing to the tiny heart on the face of the ring. "Yours looks like it's a woman's ring."

Jimmy could feel his face grow red. "It's not mine, really. I found it down by the river. I didn't want to lose it, so I stuck it on my finger," he stammered.

Lisa smiled and looked deeply into his eyes. "Then it has no special meaning for you?"

Her eyes held him and pulled him closer like a magnet. Feeling like he was drowning, he laughed nervously. "No. No special meaning."

"I thought maybe your girlfriend had given it to you."

"No."

Lisa smiled. "I know this seems like a strange thing to ask, but could I try it on? It's so pretty, and . . ."

"Sure." He tried to pull the ring from his finger, but it wouldn't budge. He looked at Lisa helplessly. "Sorry. I'm afraid it's stuck."

"Never mind, really. It was silly of me to ask." She turned and started to walk away.

Jimmy hurried after her. "Hey, wait! Maybe if I put some soap on my finger I could get it off." He didn't want her to go. He wanted to keep talking to her, keep looking at her.

Lisa hesitated. The diner's neon sign cast red shadows on her white sweater. "Do you want to come to my place?" she asked softly.

Jimmy's heart beat faster. "Okay." He thought about telling Harley that he was going with her, but he was afraid she would disappear again.

"It's not far," said Lisa.

Together, they started walking toward Summer's Road. Along the way the fir trees loomed dark and menacing. Small creatures scurried through the dried brush. Deep in the forest, an owl hooted. They hadn't gone very far when Jimmy heard the sound of a truck roaring up behind them. Turning, he was suddenly blinded by the pickup's headlights. He raised his arm to shade his eyes.

"Hey, Jimmy! What's going on?" yelled Harley, leaning his head out the pickup's window. He braked the truck inches from Jimmy's feet. "I've been looking all over for you."

Jimmy walked over to the side of the pickup. "Look, Harley. I met this girl . . . Lisa. I'm going over to her house now."

Harley gave Jimmy a long, funny look. "*What?*"

Jimmy frowned. It irritated him to

have to stand there and explain his actions. "I'll catch up with you later. I know my way back to the cabin." He turned back toward Lisa—but she was gone. Thinking she'd stepped into the shadows, he called her name. But there was no answer.

"There's no one out here, buddy. Now get in the truck," said Harley. His voice sounded worried and just a bit impatient.

"That's weird. She was just here."

"And so was Bugs Bunny," Harley mumbled quietly. He motioned for Jimmy to get in.

Reluctantly, Jimmy climbed into the truck. "Are you saying you didn't see the girl who was standing there with me?" asked Jimmy.

"That's right. The only thing I saw was your raggedy behind," answered Harley. He stomped on the gas, and the truck shot forward. "Look, Jimmy, I hate to say this, but I think you're still seeing things. You're having hallucinations—just like you did after your jeep accident."

"But Lisa is *not* a figment of my imagination!" snapped Jimmy. Maybe it was too dark for Harley to see her, he reasoned. Tomorrow, he'd find where she lived and prove Harley wrong.

Chapter 6

Jimmy smiled as Harley forked pancake number six onto his plate. He glanced at his own half-eaten breakfast. It wasn't that he didn't like the diner's food—he just wasn't hungry. He went back to staring out the window, waiting for the sheriff to arrive.

"You want to use a red wiggly today?" asked Harley.

"Uh huh," said Jimmy, wondering where the sheriff was. The diner's cook, Bob Moony, had said the sheriff always stopped by for breakfast around eight o'clock. It was after eight right now.

Harley mopped up the syrup on his plate with the last bit of pancake. "Would you like a red wiggly for dessert?" Harley teased, watching Jimmy carefully.

"No dessert for me." Jimmy didn't turn from the window.

"I might as well be talking to a wall," Harley grumbled. "I suppose you're thinking about your dream girl again? Our lady of the pool?"

Jimmy ignored Harley's sarcasm. He called across the counter to Bob, "Didn't you say the sheriff came in here at eight?"

Bob stopped cleaning the grill and squinted at the clock. "I guess he's running late today. But don't worry—he'll be in. He's a bachelor."

"What's that supposed to mean?" asked Jimmy.

"He never learned to cook. And what he does cook is so bad, you'd be hard-pressed to eat it," laughed Bob, turning back to his work.

"You don't plan on telling Ray Cox that you saw a woman floating in the pool, do you?" whispered Harley under his breath.

Jimmy hesitated. He could see the concern on Harley's face.

"I'll just ask him about Lisa. Okay?"

Harley shook his head as he stood up and pulled a few dollars from his pocket. "No, I'll get it," said Jimmy, motioning for Harley to put away his money.

Jimmy followed Harley out of the diner. He wanted to reassure his friend that he wasn't crazy, but he didn't know how. If Jimmy could find Lisa, Harley might stop worrying about him. Then maybe he could stop wondering if he was seeing things.

As they headed toward the pickup, a blue-and-white squad car slid into the parking space next to the truck. Ray Cox got out and waved.

"Getting a late start this morning, boys?" asked Ray, smiling at them.

"We didn't want to wake up the

fish too early," joked Harley.

Ray Cox grinned and glanced at the sky. "If I were you, I'd get a move on before the rain hits." Puffy white clouds like cotton balls dotted the blue sky. It didn't look like rain to Jimmy, but he didn't say anything. He waited until Harley and Ray had finished with their small talk before jumping in.

"Ray, I was wondering if you know a girl named Lisa? She said she was staying close by."

Ray stared so hard at Jimmy that it seemed like he was trying to read his mind. "That name doesn't sound too familiar. What does she look like?"

"She's beautiful," exclaimed Jimmy. Ray winked at Harley. "Uh huh."

Jimmy grinned sheepishly, realizing that he was being teased. "She's about eighteen or nineteen. Tall and thin, but not *too* thin. She has long blond hair the color of summer wheat. And she has blue, blue eyes."

"Where'd you meet this girl?" asked Ray. For some reason his voice had gone cold and hard-edged. Now it sounded like he was interrogating a suspect. He took his sunglasses from his pocket and made a show of polishing them on his shirt.

"Harley and I were shooting pool last night. I noticed her playing the jukebox. When she left, I followed her. We got to talking, and I was about to go to her place when Harley showed up. But when I turned around, she had disappeared," said Jimmy.

"*Disappeared?*" asked Ray. He held up his glasses toward the sunlight, inspecting them for smudges.

"Well, she didn't *disappear* exactly. I was talking to Harley, but when I turned around she was gone. I figured she had walked on home," said Jimmy.

"Did she say where she lived?" asked Ray, slipping on his glasses.

"No, but we were headed toward

Summer's Road," said Jimmy.

For a few minutes Ray didn't say anything. Jimmy couldn't see Ray's eyes behind the polarized shades, but he felt the man staring at him, sizing him up. "I can't keep track of all the people that come through here in the summer," Ray snapped, irritably. He turned to Harley. "What kind of flies are you using today?"

"A red wiggly. It's one that my daddy made a few years ago," said Harley. He unhooked the feather lure from his shirt pocket. As he handed the fly to Ray, he noticed the older man's ring. "Say, that ring you've got on is just like the one Jimmy found."

Jimmy held up his hand so Ray could see the ring on his little finger.

Ray glanced at the ring and then at his own. He cleared his throat. "High school fad. Everyone used to wear them. I don't know why I still wear mine. Just habit, I guess." He flashed a tight smile, then quickly turned and walked back to his squad car.

Jimmy watched Ray back the car into the street and drive off. Where was the sheriff going in such a rush? He hadn't even had his breakfast yet.

Chapter 7

Harley cupped one hand over his mouth and made a honking sound as he climbed into the pickup. In a few minutes they were heading farther down Summer's Road.

Jimmy shot Harley a questioning glance. "What are you doing?"

"Just calling geese," Harley replied, his eyes wide with amusement. He cupped his hand over his mouth and made the honking sound again.

Jimmy rolled his eyes and tried to keep from smiling. "You think we're on a wild goose chase, right?"

"We've been knocking on doors for the last hour. No one has seen anyone that resembles your dream girl, Lisa. And you know why?" asked Harley.

"No. Why?" said Jimmy, already knowing what Harley was going to say.

"Because *she doesn't exist,* man. She's only in your head," said Harley. He tapped his forehead lightly with his index finger.

Jimmy rubbed his hand across his face. Maybe Harley was right. They had been looking for a long time without any luck. He wanted to keep looking. Somehow, it seemed that his very sanity depended on finding Lisa.

"Humor me, buddy. Just a couple more houses," coaxed Jimmy, realizing that Harley was losing his patience fast.

"One more try and that's it," Harley grunted. "You told me she was staying close by. We're two miles from town already. I wouldn't call that living *close by.*" With a sigh, he turned the pickup down a gravel road.

At the end of the driveway was a redwood, A-frame house. A blond woman, her back to them, stood on the deck. Jimmy's heart raced. "Bingo!" he cried, leaping from the pickup as Harley braked to a stop. He ran up the path, and Harley followed at a distance.

When Jimmy called out a greeting, the blond woman turned and smiled. Jimmy's excitement died. The woman was middle-aged. She didn't look a thing like Lisa.

"Can I help you?"

Jimmy shoved his hands in his pockets. "I don't know. I'm looking for a girl named Lisa. She said she was staying around here."

"That name doesn't ring a bell. The people who were renting this house had a daughter. But I don't think her name was Lisa. That family left early this morning. I just came here to check on the place and make sure everything was locked up. You wouldn't believe the mess some renters make," she said.

Jimmy's glance told Harley that he

felt trapped. Smirking, Harley leaned against the side of the house.

"What did you say your friend looked like?" asked the woman.

"She's tall and slender. She has blond hair that falls to her shoulders. I think she's about eighteen or nineteen. And she has the bluest eyes you've ever seen," said Jimmy. He looked down, embarrassed.

The woman thought for a moment, and then asked, "What did you say her name was?"

Jimmy brightened. "Lisa. I don't know her last name."

"Your friend Lisa sounds just like a girl who disappeared years ago. I can't remember her name, but she was tall, slender, and had long blond hair," said the woman. She stared at the river.

"About how long ago did this girl disappear?" asked Jimmy.

The woman shook her head and

laughed. "I don't know why I even mentioned it. The girl I'm thinking of disappeared more than twenty years ago. I wish I could remember her name. They say the memory goes first," she added, laughing at herself. "Sheriff Cox would remember her name."

"Why? Was he the sheriff when the girl disappeared?" asked Jimmy, trying to connect the dots in his mind.

The woman laughed. "Oh, no. He was much too young. He was her sweetheart." She glanced at her watch, then looked at Jimmy. "I've really got to get going. I'm sorry I couldn't be of some help. Maybe your girlfriend is staying across the river. There are a lot of private homes over there."

"Yeah, maybe. Well, thanks. Thanks a lot," said Jimmy. As he walked toward Harley, he thought about what the woman had said. Could the sheriff really have had a girlfriend who looked like Lisa? The idea that the two of them were somehow related blew through his mind like a chilly wind. I really have to stop thinking like this, he told himself—or I really *will* drive myself crazy.

"Are you feeling okay, Jimmy? You look like you've seen a ghost or something," Harley said as they climbed into the truck.

"No, I'm fine." But Jimmy avoided Harley's eyes.

"Look, why don't we forget about fishing today. We could go hiking or just hang out and play some pool," said Harley, his voice full of concern.

"No!" snapped Jimmy. He bit the inside of his mouth and tried to relax. He forced himself to smile at Harley. "Let's go fishing. Isn't that what we came up here for?" As they drove off, the river roared in his ears.

Chapter 8

After an hour of fishing, Jimmy told Harley that he was going upstream to try his luck. As he walked away, he heard Harley yelling at him to stay away from the pool.

Jimmy pretended not to hear. He had no intention of staying away from the pool. He *had* to find out the truth. The puffy white clouds of the morning had grown dark and gray. The sheriff was right—a storm was brewing.

In a few minutes Jimmy was staring down into the pool. The water was as calm and flat as a pane of glass. Nothing moved beneath the surface. Glancing downriver, he saw Harley standing with his back toward him.

Holding his fishing pole between his

knees, Jimmy pulled the Irish friendship ring from his finger. Working quickly, he tied the ring to the end of his fishing line. Then he reeled the line halfway up his pole. Flicking his wrist, he sent the line flying toward the center of the pool. For just a brief moment, the ring sparkled like a drop of honey on the water. Then it sank out of sight.

"Now, we'll see what we catch with this," said Jimmy. Excited and scared at the same time, he was glad that Harley was downstream. There was no way he could explain his actions to his friend. He couldn't even explain them to himself.

When something tugged on his line, Jimmy tensed. *This is it,* he thought as he started turning the reel. The tip of the pole swung downward and then popped up. *Oh, no, the line snapped!* Jimmy cursed and looked down into the dark pool.

"How's it going?"

The voice startled Jimmy. Turning, he saw Ray Cox standing just a few feet away. "I hooked something, but it got away," said Jimmy, holding up the empty fishing line.

Ray glanced at the pool and then at the sky. He fidgeted with his belt and straightened his hat. Jimmy waited. The older man scratched his chin as if he were wrestling with a thought. Finally, he said, "You know that friendship ring you found?"

"Yes, sir."

"I was just wondering if I could, uh . . . maybe buy it from you," said Ray, avoiding Jimmy's stare.

"You could if I hadn't just lost it," said Jimmy, watching closely for the other man's reaction.

Ray looked down at the ring on his finger. "I think the ring belonged to Lisa, my high school sweetheart. We were going to get married," said Ray, his voice choking with emotion.

"What happened?" asked Jimmy, softly.

"She drowned in this pool. A freak accident. It was night, and we were clowning around. She slipped and fell in. I tried to save her, but the undertow got to her before I could reach her. I searched and searched for her body." He shook his head sadly. "I couldn't find her, though. I mean, I searched up and down this river for weeks, *months*. But I found nothing."

"Did you tell the police about what happened?" Jimmy saw the remorse on the older man's face.

"No. I just let everyone think she had disappeared. I don't know why. Maybe I just didn't want to believe it myself. That was a long time ago, but to me it still seems like it was just yesterday," Ray whispered.

Raindrops started to splash against the rocks. Jimmy watched the rain creating big circles on the water's surface. He looked at Ray and took a deep breath, trying to overcome his fear. "I think Lisa is in the pool, Ray. I think she's waiting for you," said Jimmy, speaking quickly.

Ray stared at Jimmy with disgust. He grunted. "I suppose you also believe in Santa Claus and the tooth fairy. What kind of silly nonsense are you giving me, kid?"

Speaking fast so that he wouldn't be interrupted, Jimmy told Ray what had happened and what he'd seen the last couple of days. He talked about the woman he'd found in the pool, and he talked about Lisa. At last he stopped and took a deep breath. "I know the whole thing sounds fantastic, strange—even *weird*. But how else can you explain what has been going on?" asked Jimmy, not expecting an answer.

Ray squared his shoulders and pulled himself up to his full height. "I think Harley mentioned that you had a bad accident a few months ago. He said something about a head injury . . ."

"Yeah, but that was months ago," Jimmy snapped.

"Don't get all worked up, kid. I'm not saying you're crazy. I'm just saying that maybe you aren't as well as you think you are," said Ray. "I'm going to prove to you that Lisa is not waiting for me in that pool."

Jimmy glared at Ray. Why did everyone he knew want to *prove* something to him?

Ray got on his knees and leaned over the pool. "I'm going to put my hand in this water and prove to you that there's nothing down here. Okay?" He held up his hand in Jimmy's face. On his finger was the friendship ring that Lisa had given him years before.

A chill ran down Jimmy's spine. He wanted Ray to touch the water—and yet he didn't. He hoped that Ray could prove him wrong—and yet he didn't

want to admit to himself that he had
been seeing things.

"I don't know if this is a good
idea," said Jimmy, watching closely as
Ray plunged his hand into the water.

Then, suddenly, Ray was falling,
falling into the dark waters of the pool.

Chapter 9

Horrified, Jimmy watched as Ray disappeared under the water. Then he saw the man reappear in the center of the pool. Ray's eyes were frozen with fear. Jimmy screamed at him to swim closer to the boulders. As Ray struggled toward him, Jimmy reached out. He almost had the man in his grasp when something pulled Ray back under the water. For a second, Jimmy thought he saw long blond hair streaming in the water like bright seaweed.

"Hurry! Ray's drowning!" Jimmy yelled when he saw Harley coming. There was no point in jumping in to try to save Ray. That wouldn't help. The undertow would simply pull *both* of them down to a dark and watery death.

After several seconds, Ray's head broke the surface again. Water shot from his mouth and he gulped for air. Again, Jimmy reached out to grab him. This time he caught Ray's shirt collar. "Give me your arm!" yelled Jimmy. He was afraid that if the man's shirt ripped, he would lose him for sure.

Suddenly Ray went limp, and his head fell forward. Jimmy struggled to keep the man's face out of the water. But the current was very strong and powerful, sucking Ray's body down. "Ray! Give me your arm!" Jimmy yelled again.

"He can't hear you! He's passed out!" yelled Harley, dropping down beside Jimmy.

"I've got to get a better grip," cried Jimmy. His arms trembled with the weight of the drowning man.

"Hold him!" Harley screamed as he jumped down onto a lower boulder. "Now try to swing him over in my direction," Harley ordered.

With the last of his strength, Jimmy pushed Ray's lifeless body sideways, toward Harley. "It's okay! I've got him!" cried Harley. Together, they dragged the sheriff from the water.

When they rolled Ray over on his back, they saw that his face was bloodless, his eyes blank. Jimmy bent down and checked Ray's pulse. "He's stopped breathing, and I can't find a pulse," cried Jimmy. Quickly, he lifted Ray's neck and tilted his head backward. Then he opened Ray's mouth and began administering CPR.

Harley stood by helplessly as Jimmy moved back and forth from Ray's mouth to his chest. "What can I do?" he asked nervously.

Jimmy didn't look up. If he did, he would lose the rhythm he'd created. Finally, after what seemed an eternity, Jimmy felt Ray's chest start to heave under his hands. With a grunt, he rocked back on his heels.

"He's breathing, Harley! He's *breathing*," Jimmy cried. Relief flooded his body as he watched the color return to the older man's face. Finally, Ray coughed and spat and tried to sit up.

"Here, Ray, let me help you," said Jimmy, putting his arm around the man's shoulder. Dazed and confused, Ray looked up at Jimmy as if he didn't know him.

"It's okay, you're going to be all right," Jimmy said softly.

Harley looked like he was going to be sick. "What's wrong, man?" Jimmy asked. "Ray is okay. We just have to get him back to town and into some dry clothes." Then he saw what Harley was staring at.

Jimmy felt a wave of nausea wash over him. He gagged. He saw that blood was spurting from a hole in Ray's hand. Ray's finger, his ring finger, was gone. And so was the ring.